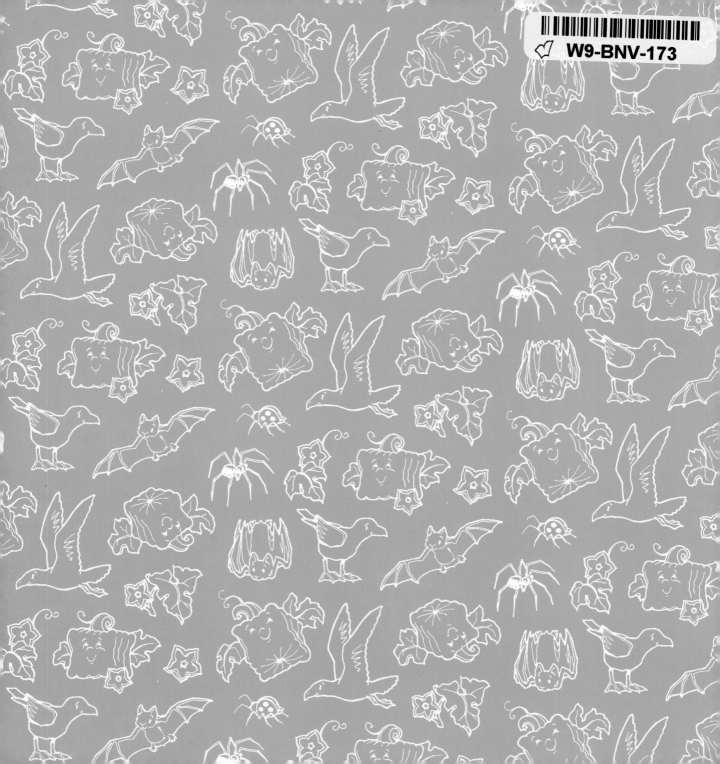

The Legend of Spookley the Square Pumpkin™

Written by Joe Troiano
Illustrated by Susan Banta

This book is dedicated to my endless source of inspiration and joy, my son, Nicholas.

BACKPACK BOOKS

2001 Barnes & Noble Books   ISBN 0-7607-2754-6   Printed and bound in Italy   10 9 8 7 6 5 4 3 2

One day in the pumpkin patch,
the strangest little pumpkin hatched.
Spookley wasn't like his friends—
where they had curves, he had ends.

Spookley was different.
He was odd,
he was rare.
Spookley the pumpkin wasn't round—
he was…square!

While the round pumpkins had fun rolling along,
poor Spookley sat there shaped all wrong.
He tried and tried with all his might,
but he couldn't budge—
he just sat tight.

The other pumpkins teased him because he was square.
Spookley wished he was round and could roll everywhere.

That is…
until one night when they all discovered,
it's fine to be round when the weather is fair,
but there are times it's better to be a square.

Halloween was just a day away,
when a mighty storm blew across the bay.
It tossed the round pumpkins to and fro.
It snapped their vines, then off they'd go.

Bouncing left.
Slamming right.
Banging!
Bashing!
What a sight!

Spookley sat there filled with fright,
but glad to be a square that night.

Suddenly, the fence gave way!
Three pumpkins rolled out and into the bay.

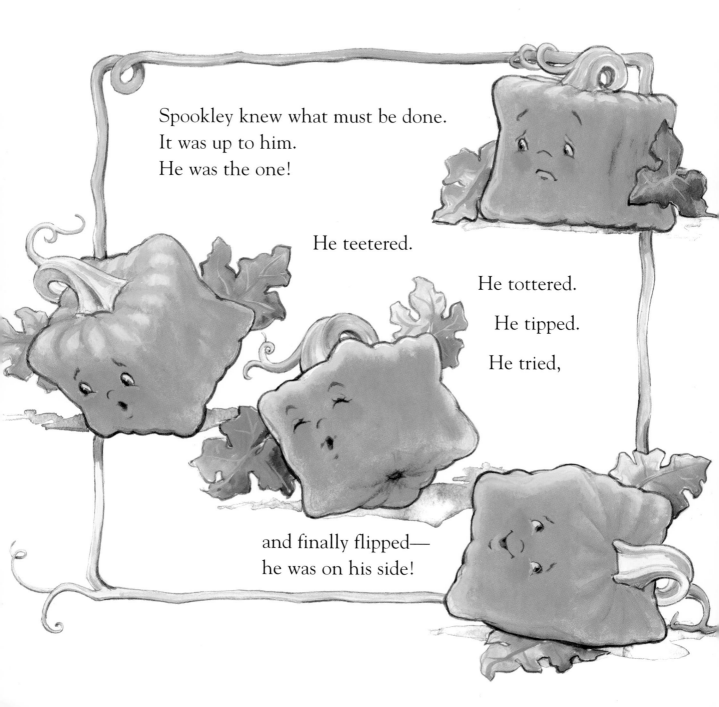

Spookley knew what must be done.
It was up to him.
He was the one!

He teetered.

He tottered.

He tipped.

He tried,

and finally flipped—
he was on his side!

Again he tipped.

Again he flopped.

Again he flipped.

And then…

He stopped—

right in the gap
where the fence had snapped.
He blocked the way.
The hole was capped.

All the pumpkins shouted, "Hooray!"
Spookley the square pumpkin had saved the day!

Then a pumpkin hit him with a whack.
He thought his shell would start to crack.
Then another one hit him with a thump,
and another one with a smack.

Then one by one,
a ton of pumpkins piled on the stack—
with a bang and a bash and a crunch and a crash,
and then…
it all went black.

At dawn, when the storm had stopped,
the farmer came out and checked his crop.
He picked his pumpkins up, one by one,
and laid them out in the warm, dry sun.

And when the last was moved away,
the farmer could see what had saved the day.
An odd-shaped pumpkin, short and dense,
was wedged against the broken fence.

Its shell was bruised,
its stem was too.
But there was brave little Spookley
sitting straight and strong and true.

Right then and there
the farmer knew—
of all the seeds he'd ever sown,
Spookley's were the most special that had ever grown.

And the next year when it was time to sow,
he sowed those seeds in every row.
He watered and weeded
and watched them grow.

And…oh!
That morning about mid-June,
when the pumpkin patch began to bloom,
there were tiny pumpkins everywhere—
hundreds and hundreds,
most of them square!

But...

some were cubes,
and some rectangular.

Some were flat,

and others triangular.

There was a bed of bright red ones
and two rows of blue.

There were polka-dot pumpkins
and rainbow ones too.

There were thousands of colors
and hundreds of shapes.
Oh, what a garden variety makes!

Now every year on Halloween
Spookley's patch is quite a scene.
People come from far and near
to see what wonders grew that year.

They stop.
They gawk.
They gaze.
They stare.

Then they pick a pumpkin
that's round, triangular,
or perfectly...square!

Now you know the story of how Spookley grew.
Maybe someday, if you tell someone too,
that someone you tell might go tell another,
and maybe one day we all will discover—
you can't judge a book,
or a pumpkin…
by its cover.